CHERISHED FAIRY TALES

Sleeping Beauty

illustrated by Jim Talbot
retold by Dandi

Once upon a time in a land far away lived a King and his Queen. Every day they prayed for a child, until finally their prayers were answered.

The King and Queen made plans for a glorious
christening, with enchanted fairies as their guests of
honor. The King engraved invitations for the famous
five fairies: Rena, Rita, Ruby, Randi (the youngest)
... and Wretch.

"Must you invite Wretch?" the Queen asked.
"That wicked fairy is such a party pooper."

The King tossed Wretch's invitation into the fire.
"Ah well, no one has heard from the Wretch in
decades."

The day of the Princess' christening, music played and servants bustled with roasts and fowl. Rena, Rita, and Ruby flew to the Princess' royal bassinet. "Now for our gifts," said Rena, the eldest.

But Randi, the youngest fairy, was hiding behind the curtains. This was her first christening, her first chance to bestow a wonderful gift. She had stayed awake the whole night and still hadn't decided what to give the young Princess.

Just then a cold wind swept through the banquet hall. The doors thrust open and in stormed a bony figure draped in black. A heavy silence fell over the guests. Although they had never met, Randi knew this must be the horrible fairy, Wretch.

"A royal feast for the Princess, and I was not invited?" Wretch seethed.

The King and Queen stammered their apologies, but the Wretch paid no attention. "Go on with your gifts," she said in a syrupy, sweet voice. "For I have a gift of my own for the Princess."

The guests relaxed, and a festival mood returned. Only young Randi remained wary. She stayed where she was, hidden by the drapes.

"To you, Sweet Princess," said Rena with a wave of her crystal wand, "the gift of beauty."

"The spirit of an angel," bequeathed Rita.

"Kindness and grace," said Ruby. And she touched the Princess with her ruby wand.

"Now for my gift," said the Wretch. The wicked
fairy drew herself to thrice her size. "Before your
sixteenth birthday, Little Princess, you shall prick your
finger on the spindle of a spinning wheel and die."
Then, with a wild and evil cackle, she disappeared,
leaving all in the room stricken with grief.

"Wait!" said Randi. "All is not lost, I still have my gift to bestow."

"What good is that?" roared the King.

"Even I could not reverse the Wretch's evil," said Rena.

"No," Randi agreed. "But this much I can do." She waved her wand over the Princess.

"If your finger, you should prick,
Neither die, nor fall you sick.
You shall sleep until the day,
True love makes its careful way."

The King ordered all spinning wheels burned. In time, as the Princess grew in beauty, grace, and charm, the Wretch's curse was nearly forgotten. The Princess brought joy to her parents and everyone, from kings to scullery maids.

On the Princess' sixteenth
birthday, the King and
Queen prepared a great celebration.
The Princess and her puppy chased each other around
the castle.

When the Princess happened upon a secret turret at
the top of the castle, she pushed against the door with
all her might. Suddenly it opened, sending her sprawling
on the floor by a wooden wheel of some sort.

The Princess looked up into the wrinkled face of an old woman, a shawl drawn over her head and shoulders.

"Oh," said the Princess, pulling herself up and examining the strange wheel. "I am so sorry, I didn't think anyone was up here. Please tell me. What is this?"

The toothless woman grinned. "It's a spinning wheel. Here, try it yourself."

"Ouch!" The Princess drew back her hand to see a drop of blood where the spindle had pricked her finger.

As she began to swoon, the Princess heard a loud cackle and saw the form of the evil Wretch.

The King and Queen knew at once what had happened. They carried their daughter to her golden bed and sent for the young fairy, Randi.

As guests below gathered for celebration, Randi made a decision. When the Princess did wake, she must find her family and friends as she had left them. With a wave of her wand, Randi cast all in the castle into a deep sleep. The King and Queen and guests in the dining hall, the servants and scullery maids in the kitchen, even the horses and pheasants dropped where they stood. And the little puppy curled peacefully next to his mistress.

Years passed. One hundred years later, a young Prince rode by and spotted the castle's tower poking through the briars.

"Pray, what is that yonder?" he asked an old woman.

The woman was none other than Randi. "Sir," said she. "One hundred years ago an evil fairy cast a spell. A Princess and all her court are trapped within."

"The Princess is a hundred years old?" asked the Prince.

"One hundred and sixteen," answered Randi. The fairy knew if this Prince were kind enough to free what he believed to be an ancient princess, he would be worthy of the Beauty within.

The Prince thanked the good fairy. "I will give my life!" And with that, he rode to the edge of the forest, drew his sword, and began hacking away at the briars.

Once inside, the Prince climbed over sleeping lords and ladies, their spoons still in air, servants snoring in stairways.

The Prince mounted the steps to the Princess' room. Amazed by her beauty, he exclaimed, "Why, you're not old. You are a Sleeping Beauty." He knelt and gently kissed her lips.

Sleeping Beauty opened her eyes and beheld the handsome Prince, the very one she had been dreaming of for a hundred years. "Finally," she said, sighing deeply. "My Prince!"

The Princess and her Prince descended the steps, her puppy nipping at their heels. The spell broken, the castle awoke. The King and Queen consented, and the birthday party transformed into a glorious wedding celebration, with Randi as the Maid of Honor.

As for gifts, the couple gladly accepted only presents that came wrapped with bows on top. And they all lived happily ever after...and got by on very little sleep.